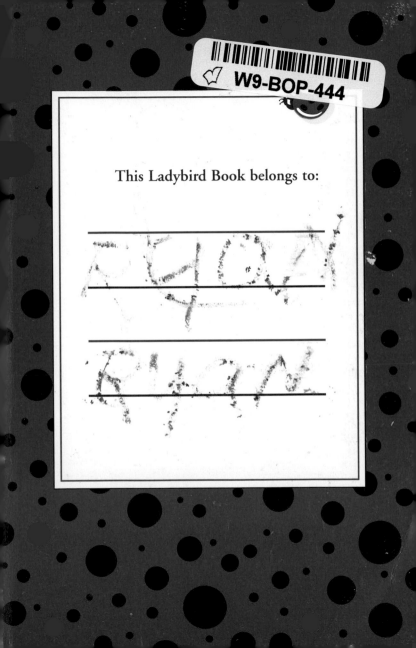

W9-BOP-444

This Ladybird Book belongs to:

Retold by Audrey Daly
Illustrated by Peter Stevenson

Cover illustration by John Gurney

Originally published in the United Kingdom by Ladybird Books Ltd © 1993

First American edition by Ladybird Books USA
An Imprint of Penguin USA Inc.
375 Hudson Street, New York, New York 10014

Printed in Great Britain
10 9 8 7 6 5 4 3 2 1

ISBN 0–7214-5627-8

FAVORITE TALES

The Gingerbread Man

nce upon a time, a little old woman and a little old man lived by themselves in a little old house by the side of the road.

One day, the little old woman decided to make a special treat.

"I will bake a gingerbread man," she said.

So the little old woman made a gingerbread man and put him in the oven to bake. But before long, she heard a tiny voice calling, "Let me out! Let me out!"

The little old woman went to the oven to listen. Then she opened the oven door.

The gingerbread man jumped right out! He skipped across the kitchen and ran out the door.

The little gingerbread man was on his way down the road before the little old woman and the little old man were out of the house. They could not run nearly as fast as he could.

"Stop! We want to eat you. Stop, little gingerbread man!" they cried, quite out of breath.

But the gingerbread man just sang,

"Run, run, as fast as you can,
You can't catch me,
I'm the gingerbread man!"

Soon the gingerbread man met a cow. "Stop, little man!" mooed the cow. "You look very good to eat!"

But the gingerbread man ran faster. And he sang as he ran,

"Run, run, as fast as you can,
You can't catch me,
I'm the gingerbread man!"

The cow ran and ran, but she could not catch the little gingerbread man.

Farther down the road, the gingerbread man met a horse. "Stop little man!" said the horse. "You look very good to eat!"

But the gingerbread man ran faster.

The horse galloped and galloped as fast as he could, but he was not fast enough to catch the gingerbread man.

"I have run from a little old woman, a little old man, a cow, and a horse," cried the gingerbread man. And he sang as he ran,

"Run, run, as fast as you can,
You can't catch me,
I'm the gingerbread man!"

The little gingerbread man ran on and on. He was very proud of his running, and quite pleased with himself.

At last he met a sly old fox. "Stop! Stop, little man," said the fox, grinning and licking his lips. "I want to talk to you."

But the gingerbread man did not stop.
He sang as he ran,

"Run, run, as fast as you can,
You can't catch me,
I'm the gingerbread man!"

The cunning old fox could run
very fast indeed, and he ran after the
gingerbread man. He followed him
into the forest.

Before too long they came to a river.
The gingerbread man did not know
what to do.

The cunning old fox was
not far behind. "I will
help you," he said. "If
you jump onto my tail,
I will take you
across. You will
be quite safe
and dry."

So the little gingerbread man jumped
onto the fox's tail and the fox began to
swim across the river.

Soon the fox said, "You are too heavy
for my tail. Jump onto my back."

The little gingerbread man jumped
onto the fox's back.

Soon after, the fox said, "Little
gingerbread man, you are too heavy for
my back. Jump onto my nose."

And the little gingerbread man
jumped onto the fox's nose.

Finally they reached the other side of
the river. The fox threw back his head
and tossed the gingerbread man
high in the air.

Down fell the
gingerbread man,
right into the
fox's mouth.

And that was the end
of the little
gingerbread
man.

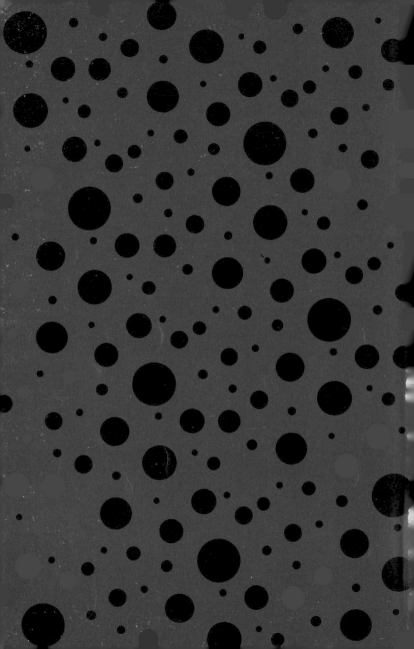